I Can Read!
Picture Book

THE WITCH WHO WAS AFRAID OF WITCHES

STORY BY ALICE LOW

PICTURES BY JANE MANNING

BARNES & NOBLE

NEW YORK

To Lila and Violet with love
—A.L.

To Gracie, my Halloween friend
—J.M.

The Witch Who Was Afraid of Witches
Text copyright © 1978 by Alice Low
Text adaptation for I Can Read Chapter Book edition copyright © 1999 by Alice Low
Illustrations copyright © 1999 by Jane Manning

This 2008 edition licensed for publication by Barnes & Noble Publishing, Inc., by
arrangement with HarperCollins Publishers.

HarperCollins Publishers® and I Can Read Books® are registered trademarks.

Previously published by Pantheon Books, a division of Random House, Inc., New York.

Barnes & Noble Publishing, Inc.
122 Fifth Avenue
New York, NY 10011

ISBN-10: 0-7607-8147-8 — ISBN-13: 978-0-7607-8147-0
Manufactured in China.
08 09 MCH 10 9 8 7 6 5 4 3

CONTENTS

· 1 ·
THE WITCH SISTERS

Wendy was the youngest witch in her family. She had the weakest witch power. And she was afraid of witches—older, bossy, mean witches like her two sisters.

Her oldest sister, Polly, *knew* everything.

She knew where to get the best sassafras wood for broomsticks and the best frogs' toes for witches' brew. And she knew the best books for witches' spells, too.

One day, Polly was going to the sassafras grove.

"Take me with you," Wendy begged.

Polly said, "You're too young. You don't even have the right kind of wood in your broomstick. You don't know anything, and you'll never learn."

Wendy's middle sister, Wog, knew how to *do* everything best.

She flew the fastest of any witch in the valley and cackled the loudest. She cackled, *"Heh, heh, heh. I'll get you,"* and she really got you. And she used her most frightening voice to make her spells work the best.

"Teach me how to say spells in that frightening voice," Wendy begged.

But Wog said, "Your voice is too weak. You don't even know how to cackle."

Wendy didn't even try to learn spells. They wouldn't work because she didn't have a frightening voice.

At night, Wendy's sisters had parties.
Wendy sat at the top of the stairs, listen-
ing to the cackles of witch laughter.

She wished she could join in.

Sometimes, Polly saw her and shouted,
"Spying again? Off with you. It's past your
bedtime."

And Wendy crept into her cold bed, hugging her broomstick.

She was afraid of the dark, afraid of witches.

Sometimes she tried to make up a spell to put on her sisters, but she needed them to tell her the right words.

"At least I have *you*," Wendy said to her broomstick. "You give me a little witch power."

Then, the day before Halloween, Wendy lost her broomstick.

Neither of her sisters would give her another. "Serves you right," they said.

Wendy felt lost without it. Now she had no witch power at all.

· 2 ·
A Ghost on the Doorstep

On Halloween night, Wendy's sisters said, "We are going to the city where there are more people to scare."

"Take me with you," Wendy said. "Please."

"How can you come with us when you don't have a broomstick?" Polly asked.

"Can't I ride with you?" asked Wendy.

"No. You would make the broomstick too heavy. Stay here, and don't let any trick-or-treaters in. They eat our candy and squirt shaving cream on the rug."

Wendy wasn't afraid of trick-or-treaters. She was much more afraid of witches.

"Turn off the lights, lock the door, and put out the fire," Polly said. "It will look like nobody is home."

Wendy did as Polly said. She sat in the dark, shivering. She wished she had her broomstick for company.

There was a knock on the door.

"Trick or treat," shouted a voice.

Wendy called, "There's nobody home."

"You're home," said a ghost on the doorstep.

"Well, I'm nobody," Wendy said.

"Is that what you are for Halloween?" asked the ghost. "Are you nobody?"

"Yes," Wendy said, "but I'm dressed as a witch."

"Why don't you come trick-or-treating with me?" asked the ghost. "I'm Roger, and my best friend, Billy, went trick-or-treating with his other best friend. Let's follow them and scare them."

"That sounds good to me," Wendy said. "Though I'm not very good at scaring people. Mostly, *I'm* scared of witches."

"You'll catch on," said Roger. "You just go woo, woo, woo."

"That's how ghosts go," Wendy said. "Witches cackle, like this, *Heh, heh, heh. I'll get you.*"

"Very good," said Roger. "You sound

like a real witch."

"Do I?" Wendy asked. "I never thought I could cackle before. But I can't be a real witch without a broomstick. I lost mine."

"If that's all you need, we have an old one at home. Come on," said Roger.

21

· 3 ·
AT ROGER'S HOUSE

They walked up a hill to Roger's house.

Roger's mother gave Wendy hot choco-
late and a candied apple and a broomstick.

Roger said, "Get on. Let's see you ride."

"I'm not any good at riding broomsticks,"
Wendy said, afraid to try. "I have no witch
power."

"Take the broomstick anyway," he said.

Wendy took the broomstick, but she didn't sit on it. This old kitchen broomstick wouldn't give her any witch power.

"Go on. Sit on it," said Roger. "It's fun."

"Okay," Wendy said. After all, Roger didn't expect her to do anything but pretend and have fun. She sat on the broomstick and said, *"Heh, heh, heh. I'll get you."* Then she gave a little jump.

She took off so fast she hit the ceiling.

"That must be a magic broomstick," said Roger. "Here, let me try it."

Roger got on and said, *"Heh, heh, heh. I'll get you."* Then he gave a little jump. But nothing happened.

"Darn it. It doesn't work," he said.

"I'll try it," said Roger's mother.

She sat on it and cackled and gave a little jump. But nothing happened again.

"I'll try it again," Wendy said.

Again, she took off easily. She zoomed around and around before she landed.

"I guess I do have a little witch power," she said. "I never thought so before. But I still don't know any spells."

"Then make one up," said Roger. "You're magic."

That made a really good spell pop into Wendy's head. She said it in a frightening voice.

"*Frogs and lizards*
Toads and newts
Buttons, raincoats
Hiking boots.

Turn this ghost
Into a witch.
Presto, change-o
Make a switch."

Roger's robes turned black.

"Great!" he said. "I wanted to be a witch, but we didn't have any black sheets. But I need a pointed hat."

29

"Oh, that's easy," Wendy said. "I don't even have to think about that one—

Stew and brew
And cat and bat.
Give this witch
A pointed hat."

"Great!" said Roger. "Now let's fly!"

"Be careful," said the new witch's mother. "Don't fly too fast."

"We won't," they said, as Wendy steered the broomstick out the window.

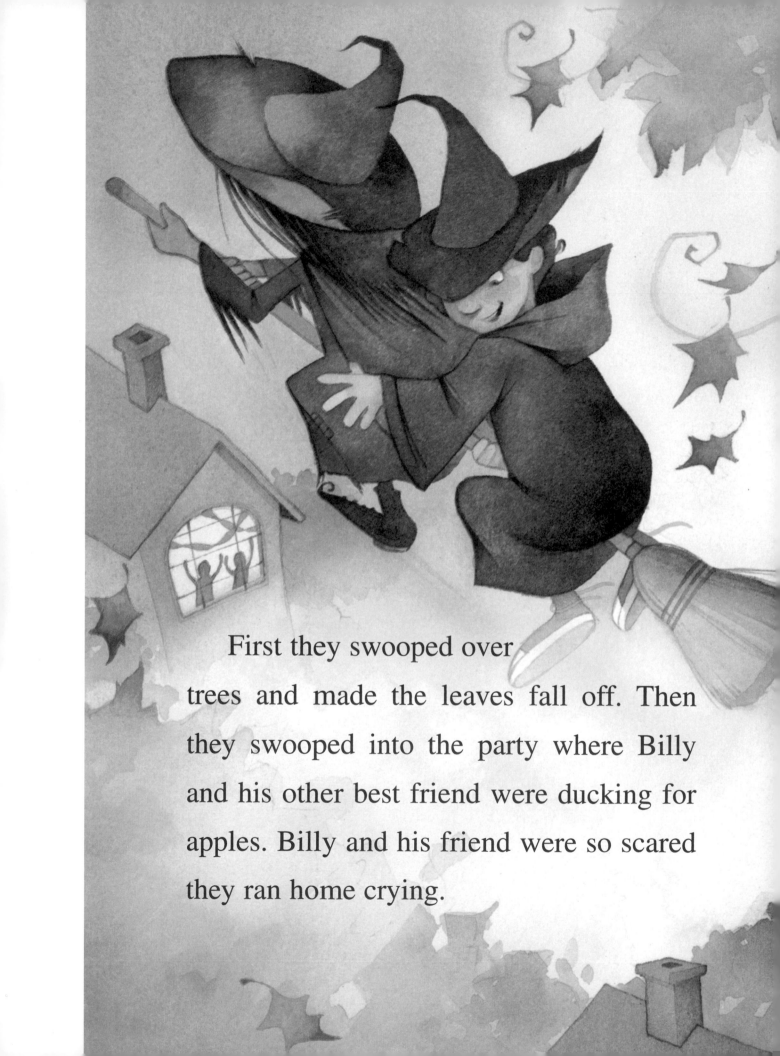

First they swooped over
trees and made the leaves fall off. Then
they swooped into the party where Billy
and his other best friend were ducking for
apples. Billy and his friend were so scared
they ran home crying.

Suddenly the clock struck midnight. "I'd better fly you home," Wendy said.

"I want to come home with you and keep on being a witch," said Roger. "You *are* a real witch, aren't you?"

"Yes, I am a real witch, with my own witch power," Wendy said. "I just found that out, and you helped. But I have to turn you back into a ghost and take you home. Your mother would miss you."

"Broiled figs
And toasted toast.
Turn this witch
Back to a ghost."

"Wow!" Roger said. "Thanks. And you
can keep the broomstick."

34

"Thanks a lot," said Wendy. "See you next Halloween."

Wendy flew home and went to sleep without worrying about witches. She wasn't afraid of witches anymore.

· 4 ·

Two Strong Spells

Wendy woke up. It was still dark outside, and her sisters weren't home yet.

"It's far too late for them to be out," she said. "They may be older, but they have no sense. I will have to teach them a thing or two."

She took her time making up two spells. They weren't as fancy as the spells her sister Polly found in books, but Wendy knew they had special power because they were her own.

"Snakes and cakes
And pumpkin pie.
Oldest sister
You can't fly.

Salt and pepper,
Bouncing ball.
Middle sister
You will fall."

"Oh dear," Wendy said. "I forgot to say the spells in a really frightening voice. I hope they work."

An hour later, her sisters came limping home. Wendy's spells had worked!

"The strangest thing happened," Polly said. "All of a sudden I couldn't take off. My broomstick was too heavy."

"I took off," Wog said, "but the wind blew my broomstick away."

"My broomstick blew away too," Polly said. "We had to walk. Ow! My feet hurt!"

Wog said, "I feel funny all over—as if I had lost my witch power. Now I know how *you* feel without your broomstick."

"That's over now," Wendy said. "I found a pretty good broomstick."

"That's just an old kitchen broomstick," Polly said.

"Well, it works for me," Wendy said.

"It couldn't possibly," said Polly.

Polly got on, but she couldn't take off, "I knew it was no good," she said.

Wog got on, but she couldn't take off either.

Then Wendy got on. She said, *"Heh, heh, heh. I'll get you,"* in her own voice. Then she gave a little jump.

Wendy zoomed out the window and back in. She had flown faster than her sisters ever had.

"How can it be?" Polly asked. "I thought I knew everything. That broom-stick isn't even made of sassafras."

"How can it be?" Wog asked. "I thought I knew how to do everything best. Wendy didn't even use a frightening voice."

Wendy felt sorry for her sisters.

"You're probably tired," she said. "Get a good sleep, and tomorrow you'll be able to fly."

In bed, Wendy made up two spells to take the spells *off* her sisters.

Oldest sister

You can fly.

All you have to do

Is try.

Middle sister

Flying's fun.

The spell I made

Is now undone.

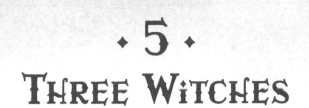

· 5 ·
THREE WITCHES

The next day they went to the sassafras grove to cut two sticks for brooms.

"This one is best," Polly said. "Now I'll be able to fly again." And she did.

Wog found another stick. She sat on it and said, "*Mumble, mumble, tumble, tumble*," in a frightening voice. "Now I'll be able to fly again." And she did.

Wendy took off too, on her old kitchen broomstick.

Wendy never told them about her spells. It was enough to know that her oldest sister thought she knew everything, but didn't. And that her middle sister thought she knew how to do everything best, but didn't.

And she never told them that she had found her own special witch power. She didn't have to.

They knew she was different.

And they treated her differently, just like one of them.